for Joshua
and his red shoes

Copyright © 1997 by Steve Lavis

CIP data available.

First published in the United States in 1998
by Lodestar Books, an affiliate of Dutton Children's Books,
a member of Penguin Putnam Inc.,
375 Hudson Street, New York, New York 10014

Originally published in Great Britain in 1997
by Ragged Bears Limited, Hampshire, England

Printed in Hong Kong   ISBN 0-525-67578-7
First American Edition   10 9 8 7 6 5 4 3 2 1

Steve Lavis

JUMP!

Lodestar Books

Dutton   New York

Tiger jumping,
frog jumping,
let's jump too.

Monkey swinging,
teddy swinging,
let's swing too.

Lion roaring,
teddy soaring,
let's roar too.

ROAR!

Snake slithering,
teddy shivering,
we're not scared of you!

Toucans flying,
frog trying,
teddy flying too.

Elephant stamping,
frog stamping,
let's stamp too.

Giraffe munching,
frog jumping,
we're as tall as you!

Crocodile snapping, let's start clapping, frog's scared of you.

Help!

Tiger marching,
monkey dancing,
elephant marching
too.

Lion marching, crocodile marching, let's all march with you.

STOP that marching,
STOP that dancing,
I've just shouted ...